VALERIAN spatiotemporal agent

WELCOME TO ALFLOLOL

BY J.C. MEZIERES AND P. CHRISTIN

COLOR: E. TRAN-LE
TRANSLATION: S. BAKER

DARGAUD INTERNATIONAL PUBLISHING INC.

535 Fifth Avenue, New York, N.Y. 10017

TITLES AVAILABLE

AMBASSADOR OF THE SHADOWS
WORLD WITHOUT STARS
WELCOME TO ALFLOLOL

© DARGAUD Editeur 1972

All translation, reproduction and adaptation rights strictly reserved
for all countries including the USSR and excepting Canada and USA

Legal deposit 1st quarter 1983 N° 3311

I S B N 2-205-06951-9

Printed in Italy by Fratelli Pagano (Genoa)

English language text © DARGAUD CANADA LTD. 1983

307 Benjamin Hudon, St-Laurent, Montreal, P.Q. H4N 1J1

All translation, reproduction and adaptation rights
strictly reserved for Canada and USA

I S B N 2-205-06951-9

First Edition 1983

TECHNOROG! VAST PLANET OF INEXHAUSTIBLE RESOURCES. ONE OF THE CENTRAL NERVE CENTERS OF THE TERRAN GALACTIC EMPIRE. HERE RARE METALS DESTINED FOR THE EMPIRE'S SPACECRAFT ARE EXTRACTED, HERE THE MAGNETIC SALTS WHICH FUEL THE ULTRA-LIGHT MOTORS ARE STORED, AND HERE THE HEAVY EQUIPMENT DESTINED FOR THE OTHER PLANETS UNDER EARTH'S CONTROL IS ASSEMBLED.

TECHNOROG! WORLD WITH A HARSH CLIMATE, WHERE THE PITILESS SIROCCO WINDS OFTEN BLOW FROM THE DESERT, BUT WITH ADMIRABLE FORESTS, STRANGE OCEANS WITH BRIGHTLY COLORED WAVES, AND IMPRESSIVE MOUNTAINS.
FOR PURPOSES OF INTENSIVE DEVELOPMENT MEN HAVE SETTLED THIS OTHERWISE UNINHABITED WORLD, THAT IS, EXCEPT FOR VARIOUS SPECIES OF GIGANTIC ANIMALS — INOFFENSIVE AS LONG AS YOU LEAVE THEM ALONE..

PROTECTED BY EARTH'S IMPOSING TECHNOLOGICAL MACHINERY, SHELTERED UNDER DOMES WHICH REPRODUCE THE CYCLE OF DAY AND NIGHT, THEY KNOW NOTHING OF THE WORLD WHICH SURROUNDS THEM, OF THE SLOW RHYTHM OF DARKNESS AND LIGHT WHICH EVERY THIRTY TERRAN DAYS PLUNGES THE PLANET INTO OBSCURITY FOR THE DURATION OF A LUNAR MONTH. ABSOLUTE MASTERS OF THE SOIL WHICH THEY EXPLOIT, THEY WORK ON ... COLONISATION, WHICH NOW GOES BACK ALMOST TWO CENTURIES, HAS NEVER ENCOUNTERED ANY PROBLEMS, AND THE FEW VESTIGES OF AN ANCIENT RACE, APPARENTLY EXTINCT FOR THOUSANDS OF YEARS, HAVE BEEN TRANSFERRED TO THE SPACE MUSEUM AT GALAXITY... BACK ON FARAWAY EARTH...

THIS IS THE WORLD FAST BEING LEFT BEHIND BY ONE OF THE SPATIOTEMPORAL SERVICE'S SHIPS WHICH IS NOW APPROACHING THE ASTEROID BELT SURROUNDING TECHNOROG ...

... A SHIP BELONGING TO TWO OF THE SERVICE'S YOUNG AGENTS, VALERIAN AND LAURELINE, WHO ARE GETTING READY TO RETURN TO EARTH UPON COMPLETION OF THEIR INSPECTION MISSION ON TECHNOROG.

PHEW! AM I GLAD TO BE GETTING OUT OF THAT PLACE! WHAT A DISMAL BUNCH DOWN THERE!... IT'S UNBELIEVABLE THAT ANYONE COULD LIKE WORK THAT MUCH!

THAT'S UNFAIR, LAURELINE! TECHNOROG HAS THE BEST ENGINEERS IN THE EMPIRE. WITHOUT THEM, YOU WOULDN'T BE SITTING HERE COMFORTABLY WAITING TO MAKE THE BIG LEAP TO GALAXITY WITHOUT LIFTING A FINGER!

BESIDES, THEY'RE ALL VOLUNTEERS! TECHNOROG IS THE SPEARHEAD OF TERRAN INDUSTRY...

OKAY, OKAY! SAVE THE OFFICIAL SONG AND DANCE FOR YOUR INSPECTION REPORT. YOU'D BE BETTER OFF PAYING ATTENTION TO YOUR PILOTING IN THIS RUBBLE!

HMM... YOU'RE PROBABLY RIGHT. WE'RE APPROACHING THE REEFS. I'LL ASK THEM TO OPEN THE PROTECTIVE SHIELD.

CIRCULATING PRUDENTLY AMONG THE REEFS, MANEUVERING THROUGH THE CHANNEL MARKED BY ELECTRO-MAGNETIC RELAY BEACONS WHICH ENCLOSE TECHNOROG IN AN UNASSAILABLE PROTECTIVE NETWORK...

TECHNOPORT? VALERIAN HERE. SHIP XB 982. WE'RE NEARING CHANNEL NUMBER EIGHT. REQUEST OPENING OF PROTECTIVE SHIELD.

TECHNOPORT HERE. REQUEST GRANTED. GO AHEAD, XB 982.

VALERIAN HEADS HIS CRAFT FOR FREE SPACE
WHILE THE SHIELD, OPEN AN INSTANT, CLOSES
BEHIND HIM.

GOOD! THE SPATIOTEMPORAL
COORDINATES ARE SET,
WE CAN MAKE
THE JUMP TO EARTH
NOW.
READY,
LAURELINE?

LAURELINE

LAURELINE,
WHAT'S
WRONG?

VALERIAN! IT'S ...
IT'S SO STRANGE ...
I FELT A SORT OF
CALL, A CRY
OF DESPAIR ...

THERE'S SOMEBODY OR
SOMETHING NEAR US.
AND THAT SOMETHING
NEEDS OUR
HELP ...
I COULD
FEEL
IT!

HOLY COMETS! IF THERE'S REALLY
SOMETHING THERE, WE SHOULD
BE ABLE TO DETECT IT.
GO OVER TO THE SCREENS
WHILE I KEEP ALONGSIDE
THE SHIELD ...

... FOR WHAT SEEMS AN ETERNITY SHE SEARCHES THROUGH SPACE IN VAIN WHEN ...

VALERIAN! THERE! STRAIGHT AHEAD!

GOT IT. I'LL HEAD FOR IT!

WHAT AN ODD STRUCTURE!

IT'S A SHIP IN DISTRESS! LOOK, IT'S FALLING TOWARDS THE PROTECTIVE SHIELD!

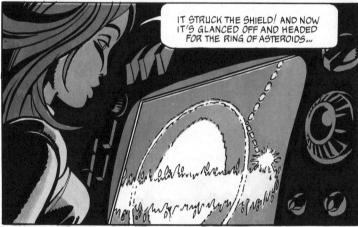

IT STRUCK THE SHIELD! AND NOW IT'S GLANCED OFF AND HEADED FOR THE RING OF ASTEROIDS...

RIGHT... EVEN I CAN'T GO ANY FARTHER... IT'S TOO DANGEROUS!

IT'S ALL OVER, THE SHIP'S CRASHED!

THE SAME THING WILL HAPPEN TO US IF I KEEP GOING. WE'LL HAVE TO STAY IN ORBIT HERE AND GO OUT TO EXAMINE THE WRECK.

WHAT'S STRANGE IS THAT THERE WAS NO OTHER CALL FOR HELP. DO YOU THINK THAT THE ... UH ... PEOPLE ON THE SHIP WERE KILLED IN THE COLLISION?

LEAVING THEIR CRAFT, VALERIAN AND LAURELINE FLOAT LIGHTLY THROUGH THE ETHER AND, SLIPPING IN AMONG THE TANGLE OF ROCKS...

... THEY FINALLY REACH THE AREA AROUND THE MYSTERIOUS, PARTIALLY-RENT VESSEL...

UP THERE .... THAT MUST BE THE PILOT'S STATION!

AND THIS MUST BE THE LIVING QUARTERS FOR THE VESSEL'S OCCUPANTS ... BUT THEY'RE COMPLETELY EMPTY...

HMMM... IN ANY CASE, THIS IS AN EXTRA-TERRESTRIAL SHIP! SINCE EVERYTHING IS OPEN, WE CAN ASSUME THEY DON'T BREATHE OXYGEN... FROM THE SIZE OF THESE THINGS, THOSE BEINGS MUST BE ENORMOUS...

YES ... THEY MUST ALSO HAVE A HEARTY APPETITE. COME LOOK!

THEIR FOOD RESERVES!

EMPTY AS WELL ... THEY RAN OUT OF FOOD. DO YOU THINK MAYBE THAT'S WHY THEY WERE TRYING TO APPROACH TECHNOROG, LAURELINE?

LAU...

OH NO!

NOT AGAIN! THAT GIRL HAS A GIFT FOR GETTING HERSELF INTO IMPOSSIBLE SITUATIONS!

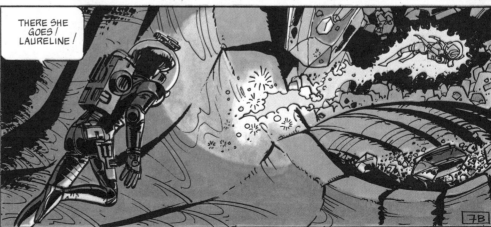

THERE SHE GOES! LAURELINE!

9

11

WATCH OUT! THIS IS A DEADLY WEAPON!

AH! WE THOUGHT WE COULD FEEL A SECOND MIND! KEEP CALM, FRIEND...

WE WISH NO HARM TO THE OTHER LITTLE BEING, ON THE CONTRARY! WE KNOW IT CAME HERE TO HELP US...

BUT OUR ANCESTOR GAROL, SHE-WHO-HAS-THE-GIFT-OF-TAKING-OVER-MINDS, IS NEARING DEATH. IN HER TERRIBLE SLEEP SHE CAN NO LONGER FREE THE LITTLE BEING SHE CALLED...

THAT'S HER?... SHE'S SERIOUSLY WOUNDED...

YES! SHE WAS STRUCK BY ROCKS WHEN OUR GREAT VESSEL FOUNDERED AGAINST THEM AND...

MAYBE I CAN SAVE HER IF YOU CAN BRING US BACK TO MY SHIP. BUT HOW ARE WE...

MY WIFE ORGAL HAS THE GIFT-OF-MAKING-THINGS-MOVE-THROUGH-SPACE. SHE IS THE ONE WHO DREW YOUR LITTLE BEING TO US. IT'S SHE WHO MADE OUR SHIP SAIL THROUGH SPACE. MAYBE SHE WILL BE ABLE TO TAKE ALL OF US.

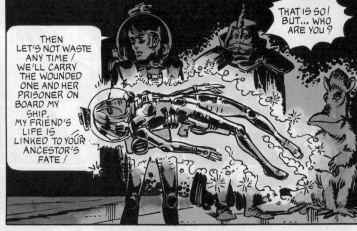

THEN LET'S NOT WASTE ANY TIME! WE'LL CARRY THE WOUNDED ONE AND HER PRISONER ON BOARD MY SHIP. MY FRIEND'S LIFE IS LINKED TO YOUR ANCESTOR'S FATE!

THAT IS SO! BUT... WHO ARE YOU?

VALERIAN, A HUMAN FROM THE FAR-OFF PLANET EARTH.

MY NAME IS ARGOL, HE-WHO-HAS-THE-GIFT-OF-SPEAKING-IN-MINDS...

I'LL TRANSLATE MY FAMILY'S WORDS FOR YOU... THOSE TWO ARE MY CHILDREN, THEY HAVEN'T DISCOVERED THEIR GIFTS YET...

AND THE ANIMAL IS OUR PET GOUMOUN. HE'S THE ONE WHO SENSED YOUR PRESENCE!...

THEN, IN THE COLD SILENCE OF SPACE, A STUPEFIED VALERIAN SEES THE LITTLE SHIP SLOWLY RISE ...

... AND POWERED SOLELY BY THE FORCE OF ORGAL'S INTENSE GAZE FIXED ON A MYSTERIOUS POINT AHEAD, AND SEEMINGLY PALPITATING WITH ENERGY ...

... HEAD SMOOTHLY TOWARDS HIS CRAFT.

THERE! YOU CAN TALK NOW!

INCREDIBLE ... SO THIS IS HOW THAT HUGE SHIP OF YOURS WORKED?

OF COURSE ... IN THE DAWN OF TIME OUR ANCESTORS PULLED THESE SHIPS FROM THE SOIL OF OUR WORLD. NOW THERE ARE NO OTHERS TO BE FOUND. WE USED OURS TO VISIT HUNDREDS OF WORLDS BEFORE COMING BACK AND CRASHING ON ALFLOLOL ...

WHAT DO YOU MEAN ON ALFLOLOL?

13

A LITTLE FARTHER...

14

LEAVING THE LITTLE SHIP, VALERIAN ENTERS HIS CRAFT AND A FEW SECONDS LATER ARGOL AND HIS PEOPLE ARE ABOARD.

LONG MINUTES LATER ...

15

LAURELINE!
MY LITTLE LAURELINE!!!

MY LITTLE LAURELINE ... NAH NAH NAH ... YOU MIGHT AS WELL HAVE FORGOTTEN ALL ABOUT ME !...

BUT...

OH, DROP IT! LUCKILY THERE ARE OTHERS WHO LOVE ME MORE THAN YOU DO...

LAURELINE !!! I SWEAR ...

FRIEND, OUR ANCESTRESS THANKS YOU THROUGH ME. SHE FEELS MUCH BETTER! OUR FRIENDSHIP WILL BE ETERNAL!

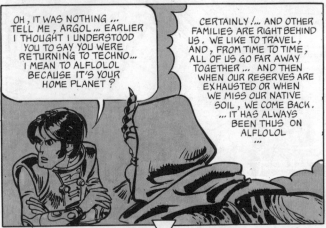

OH, IT WAS NOTHING ... TELL ME, ARGOL ... EARLIER I THOUGHT I UNDERSTOOD YOU TO SAY YOU WERE RETURNING TO TECHNO... I MEAN TO ALFLOLOL BECAUSE IT'S YOUR HOME PLANET?

CERTAINLY !... AND OTHER FAMILIES ARE RIGHT BEHIND US. WE LIKE TO TRAVEL, AND, FROM TIME TO TIME, ALL OF US GO FAR AWAY TOGETHER ... AND THEN WHEN OUR RESERVES ARE EXHAUSTED OR WHEN WE MISS OUR NATIVE SOIL, WE COME BACK. ...IT HAS ALWAYS BEEN THUS ON ALFLOLOL ...

BUT WHAT I CAN'T UNDERSTAND IS HOW OUR SHIP WAS WRECKED. THERE'S SOME NEW THING HERE THAT DREW US LIKE ...

POOR ARGOL! THAT NEW THING, AS YOU CALL IT, IS THE PROTECTIVE SHIELD AROUND TECHNOROG. I'LL EXPLAIN ...

VALERIAN!
A CALL FROM TECHNOROG! THEY'RE FURIOUS AND DEMAND TO KNOW WHY WE'RE STAYING IN THE CHANNEL AREA !... APPARENTLY IT'S DANGEROUS ...

HMMM ... THIS CALLS FOR A QUICK DECISION ... **PUT A CALL THROUGH TO THE GOVERNOR, TOP PRIORITY!**

AS THEY PASS OVER THE
ENORMOUS FLOATING STATIONS
IN MAGNET OCEAN ...

... THE GIGANTIC MINES IN THE MOUNTAINS ...

... THE COLOSSAL FACTORIES INSTALLED ON THE PLAINS ...

... AND THE PERFECTLY REGULAR HYDROPONIC PLANTATIONS ...

STUPEFACTION REIGNS AMONG THE
SPACECRAFT'S PASSENGERS ...

BUT...
WHAT HAS
HAPPENED TO
OUR WORLD ?
I NO
LONGER
RECOGNIZE IT !...

WHAT YOU SEE
HERE IS EARTH AND
HER CIVILIZATION
AT WORK, ARGOL.

18

19

I HAVE AN AUDIENCE WITH THE GOVERNOR. LET ME THROUGH...

YOU, FINE! YOUR FRIENDS, NO! SANITARY CONTROL FOR ALL FOREIGNERS!

FOREIGNERS! US! THEY'RE THE ONES WHO ARE...

DROP IT, FRIEND... DO WHAT THEY TELL YOU, YOU'LL MAKE MY TASK EASIER!

AND THAT ANIMAL THERE! THE DOOR RESERVED FOR GALACTIC LIVESTOCK!

OUR GOUMOUN!!!

I'LL GO WITH HIM AND MEET YOU AFTERWARDS...

AGENT VALERIAN, THERE'S A CRAFT WAITING FOR YOU.

I'M GOING. I'M GOING.

AND WHILE VALERIAN ENTERS TECHNOROG-VILLE'S ENCLOSURE...

LET'S GO, HURRY IT UP, SCUM!

...INSIDE TECHNOROG, THE USUAL SIGHTS AWAIT VALERIAN...

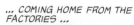

... COMING HOME FROM THE FACTORIES ...

... PREPARING TO GO OUT TO MAGNET OCEAN...

... OR RETURNING HOME FROM THE PLANTATIONS.

WHEN VALERIAN LEAVES THE INDUSTRIAL ZONES FOR THE LEISURE ZONES , HE FINALLY SPOTS THE ENORMOUS ADMINISTRATIVE BUILDING WHICH , FROM THE SUMMIT OF TECHNOROG'S CENTRAL HILL , DOMINATES THE CITY.

INDEED, A FEW SECONDS LATER, AT THE TOP OF THE MONUMENTAL EDIFICE ...

SO , AGENT VALERIAN ! YET ANOTHER OF YOUR WHIMS !! WHY DID YOU TAKE SO LONG TO RETURN TO TECHNOVILLE ? I'M WORRIED AND I'VE BETTER THINGS TO DO THAN WAIT AROUND FOR YOU !

NEVERTHELESS, YOU'RE GOING TO HAVE TO SIT STILL A MOMENT AND LISTEN TO ME. **TECHNOROG'S FORMER INHABITANTS HAVE RETURNED!!**

YOU MUST BE JOKING! THIS PLANET HAS BEEN UNOCCUPIED BY ANY SENTIENT RACE FOR OVER 4000 YEARS. TERRAN SCIENTISTS HAVE....

HEE HEE HEE! EXACTLY! THE ALFLOLOLIANS, THAT'S WHAT THEY CALL THEMSELVES, TOOK A TRIP, THAT'S ALL. AND THE REMAINS AND OTHER OBJECTS FOUND BY OUR RESEARCHERS BELONG TO THEIR ANCESTORS, BUT THEY'RE VERY MUCH ALIVE!

AND... AND HOW MANY OF THEM ARE THERE?

I BROUGHT BACK A FAMILY OF FIVE IN MY CRAFT...

FIVE? OH, GOOD, IN THAT CASE EVERYTHING WILL WORK OUT FINE.

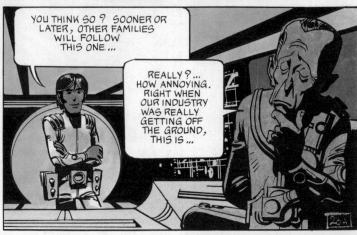

YOU THINK SO? SOONER OR LATER, OTHER FAMILIES WILL FOLLOW THIS ONE...

REALLY?... HOW ANNOYING. RIGHT WHEN OUR INDUSTRY WAS REALLY GETTING OFF THE GROUND, THIS IS...

ANNOYING OR NOT, YOU KNOW THE GALACTIC CODE, I TRUST. AFTER ALL, IT WAS GALAXITY THAT SET UP THE CODE, TO ITS EVERLASTING CREDIT.

YES, CERTAINLY... BUT THE CODE HAS NEVER BEEN APPLIED IN A SIMILAR CASE...

...THIS IS THE FIRST TIME A NATIVE POPULATION HAS BEEN FOUND **AFTER** A PLANET HAD BEEN COLONIZED BY EARTH AND...

COME ON NOW! CALL GALAXITY IF YOU WISH, BUT THEY'LL TELL YOU THE SAME THING. THE ALFLOLOLIANS HAVE THE RIGHT TO RETURN TO THE LAND THAT'S THEIRS...

AND... AHEM... DO THEY SEEM HOSTILE, THESE ALF, AFLOL... WHAT DID YOU CALL THEM?

THE ALFLOLOLIANS? HOSTILE?... NO NOT AT ALL!

MY DEAR VALERIAN, THAT'S EXCELLENT NEWS ... THEN WE'LL BE ABLE TO NEGOCIATE, WON'T WE?

HUH ... THEY'RE NOT HOSTILE, BUT THEY'RE VERY BIG, VERY STRONG, VERY INTELLIGENT, AND THEY HAVE SOME VERY STRANGE POWERS...

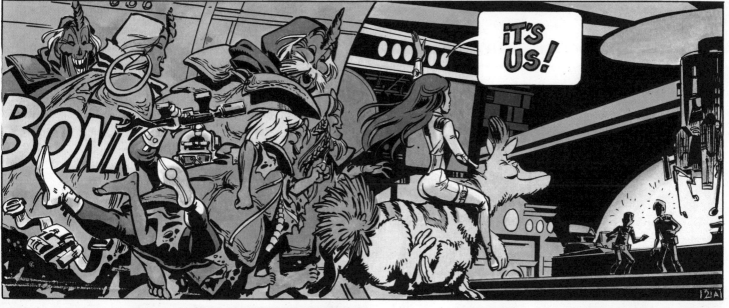

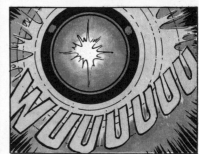

THAT'S EASY. ALL YOU HAVE TO DO IS DEMOLISH YOUR BUILDING AND DIG DOWN DEEP ENOUGH...

YES, THE TOMBS OF OUR VERY ANCIENT FAMILY ARE BURIED UNDER THIS HILL...

VALERIAN! YOU'RE NOT GOING TO LET THEM DO THAT!

UM... I'M AFRAID, GOVERNOR, THAT YOU HAVE NO CHOICE. THE GALACTICAL CODE IS CATEGORICAL.

AND, IN THE ARTIFICIAL EVENING OF A HARD-WORKING TECHNOROG SLUMBERING UNDER ITS PROTECTIVE DOME, UNEXPECTED NOISES RING OUT FROM THE SUMMIT OF THE ADMINISTRATIVE PALACE...

... WHERE, BREAKING WITH THE FUNCTIONAL FRIGIDITY OF THE PLACE, THE ALFLOLOLIANS HAVE SET UP CAMP...

FRIENDS! WHAT JOY TO HAVE YOU AMONG US! WE ARE GOING TO HOLD A FITTING CELEBRATION OF OUR RETURN TO LOVELY ALFLOLOL!

WATCH IT, CHILDREN, DON'T BREAK TOO MANY THINGS, THE TERRANS AREN'T LIKE US, THEY SEEM TO ATTACH MORE IMPORTANCE TO MATERIAL THINGS THAN WE DO ...

IF YOU CATCH ME YOU GET A KISS!

CRAAK

UH-OH! NOT AGAIN! VALERIAN'S GOING TO BE MAD. THAT BOY'S ENTIRELY TOO SERIOUS.

BUGS ME ... SHE'S STARTING TO BUG ME ... AND I'M TIRED OUT ...

FIVE DAYS OF CELEBRATING. I'M BEAT ...

OH, VALERIAN ... YOU'RE WANDERING THE HALLS TOO ...

DON'T THOSE PEOPLE EVER SLEEP?

YES, OF COURSE ... OF COURSE THEY DO ... A FEW SECONDS HERE, A FEW SECONDS THERE ... THAT'S ALL THE SLEEP THEY NEED ...

OH REALLY? WELL, I'M GOING TO GO TAKE A REST. THE WORST OF IT IS THAT I CAN'T GET ANY WORK DONE WITH ALL THIS RACKET ...

WORK? THEY OBVIOUSLY DON'T UNDERSTAND THE MEANING OF THE WORD. SO HOW CAN YOU EXPECT THEM TO LET YOU WORK?

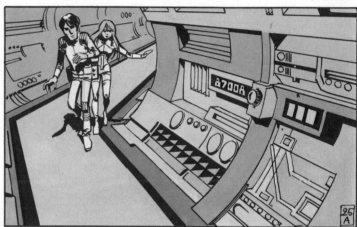

BE THAT AS IT MAY, WE CAN'T LET THIS SITUATION CONTINUE! AS THE MAN RESPONSIBLE FOR THE MINES, I MUST PROTEST!

AND WHAT ABOUT ME, THE GENERAL DIRECTOR OF PRODUCTION FOR ALL OF TECHNOROG'S FACTORIES? I MUST WARN YOU TO BE CAREFUL...

DISORDER, MY YOUNG FRIENDS! DISORDER!! I ASK YOU, WHAT COULD BE WORSE FOR PRODUCTION?

THIS WHOLE SITUATION IS INADMISSIBLE! AT LEAST BEFORE, WE KNEW WHAT THEY WERE DOING AND WHERE THEY WERE / THEY MUST BE BROUGHT BACK. AN EXPEDITION IS READY.

YOU'RE CRAZY! YOUR AFFAIRS DON'T CONCERN THEM! WHY DON'T YOU JUST LEAVE THEM ALONE ...

YOU HAVE A SUBVERSIVE ATTITUDE, YOUNG LADY! BUT YOU, VALERIAN, YOU AT LEAST UNDERSTAND THAT TECHNOROG'S INDUSTRIAL POTENTIAL IS AT STAKE HERE DON'T YOU? TECHNOROG IS AN INDUSTRIAL PLANET, NOT AN ADVENTURER'S CAMP. WHICH IS WHY WE LACK PEOPLE LIKE YOU AND WHY YOU'RE GOING TO LEAD THE EXPEDITION ...

ME? UH, YOU KNOW ...

THEY'RE HEADING FOR THE DENSE FOREST SEPARATING TECHNOROG-VILLE AND MAGNET OCEAN ... THEY'VE LEFT TRACKS. BUT NOW IT'S IMPOSSIBLE TO LOCATE THEM BY AIR, THE AIRBORNE PROBE DOESN'T RESPOND ...

YOU MUST GO AFTER THEM BY LAND. THIS IS AN ORDER ...

IN THAT CASE ...

ALWAYS DUTY FIRST, EH? ...

THAT'S ENOUGH! BETTER US THAN SOMEONE ELSE, ISN'T IT?

MMM ... MAY BE SO. BUT THAT FOREST IS THE ONE ARGOL AND HIS PEOPLE CALL ANANIL. I THINK THEY'LL BE PRETTY HARD TO FOLLOW ...

I ACCEPT.

GLAD TO SEE YOU COME TO YOUR SENSES. LET'S NOT WASTE ANY MORE TIME ...

AND A LITTLE WHILE LATER...

WHAT ABOUT ALL THE GUARDS?

THEY'VE REGAINED CONSCIOUSNESS BUT DON'T REMEMBER WHAT HAPPENED...

THE MOST MODERN EQUIPMENT AND THE MOST QUALIFIED OFFICERS HAVE BEEN GATHERED TOGETHER FOR YOUR EXPEDITION ...

BAH, YOU'RE TOO KIND !!! BUT ENOUGH CHIT-CHAT, SINCE WE HAVE TO, **LET'S GO!**

29

MUCH LATER...

MUCH FARTHER...

FARTHER STILL...

CAN WE GET GOING OR WHAT?

IMPOSSIBLE! WE CAN'T GET STARTED, THE MOSS HAS EATEN EVERYTHING!!

THE LAST SEARCH VEHICLE MADE A WRONG MOVE AND...

WE'LL KEEP ON GOING!

AAH!!!

DO SOMETHING !!!!

OUR LAST ABLE-BODIED MEN ARE PRISONERS OF THAT CARNIVOROUS PLANT! WE'LL HAVE TO FREE THEM AND THEN TURN BACK!

YOU'RE RIGHT!

ALL YOUR HARDWARE'S USELESS AND YOUR GUARDS AREN'T MUCH BETTER! YOU THERE, FREE THOSE MEN AND TAKE THEM BACK...

AND WE'LL KEEP ON, WON'T WE, VALERIAN?

YEAH, WE'RE GOING TO KEEP GOING... WITH OUR ONLY EQUIPMENT A FAULTY DETECTOR AND A SILENT MICRO-RADIO COMPLETELY STIFLED BY THIS DAMN JUNGLE...

COME ON! I'M SURE WE'LL FIND THEM!

WHILE THE JUNGLE THICKENS AROUND THEM, AND AFTER HOURS AND HOURS OF WALKING ...

WELL, WHAT'S THE DETECTOR SAY?

IT INDICATES A WEAK PRESENCE, BUT THAT COULD BE ANYTHING ... THE TRACE IS SO OLD ...

LOOK AT THE MAP ... WE CROSSED THE FOREST AT ITS NARROWEST POINT. I'M SURE THAT THEY TOOK THE SAME PATH TO GET TO MAGNET OCEAN.

NO DOUBT. WE'LL FIND OUT. WE'RE QUITE CLOSE TO THE SHORE NOW ...

BUT FIRST ... LET'S MAKE CAMP, GET SOME SLEEP AND RECUPERATE A BIT. WE'VE BEEN ALONE AND ON THE MARCH FOR OVER 48 HOURS ...

WHATEVER YOU SAY.

AND ...

SUDDENLY ...

VALERIAN! IT'S CARRYING ME OFF!

INCREDIBLE! SHE'S GETTING HERSELF HIGH-JACKED BY ANOTHER MONSTER! THIS IS BECOMING A HABIT! MY WEAPON ... QUICK!

I CAN'T AIM! I'M AFRAID I'LL HIT LAURELINE ... AND WHERE IS THAT BEAST TAKING HER?

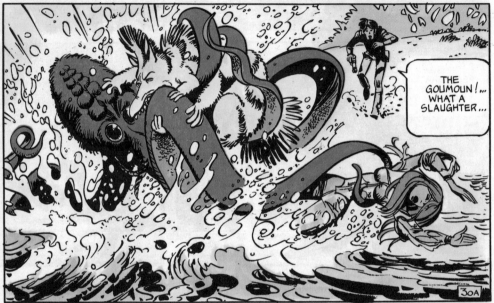

AND SOON...

WHAT BOTHERS ME ARE THOSE FLOATING HOUSES, LET'S HOPE THERE ARE STILL FURUTZ HERE ...

THOSE ARE MAGNET OCEAN'S SALT EXTRACTION PLANTS. WE MUST BE CAREFUL TO STEER CLEAR OF THEM...

LOOK, LAGOR ... A HERD OF FURUTZ! LED BY THE STRONGEST MALE. HE'S THE ONE WHO WILL LEAD THE COMBAT AND HE'S THE ONE YOU'LL HAVE TO HIT.

DON'T WORRY, THOSE THINGS ARE OF NO INTEREST TO US! HEY ... BUT... **OVER THERE !**

BUT EVEN AS THE HUNT BEGINS AMID THE FAMILY'S JOYOUS CRIES...

LOOK HOW HAPPY THEY ARE ... AND STAY ON COURSE! ARGOL ENTRUSTED THE HELM TO YOU.

I'M DOING THE BEST I CAN!!!

... BUT I'M SMALLER THAN HE IS...

AGENT VALERIAN ...

OH GREAT! LOUSY RADIO! WHAT A MOMENT TO...

RAISE YOUR HEAD, AGENT VALERIAN ...

WHILE ARGOL AND HIS FOLK GO ON WITH THE HUNT, INDIFFERENT TO THE DELUGE OF FIRE OPENING UP BEFORE THEM ...

... ALL HELL BREAKS LOOSE ON THE FURUTZ HERD, ABANDONED BY ITS OLD GUIDE ...

BUT THE EFFECT OBTAINED IS NOT AT ALL WHAT WAS EXPECTED AND, WITHIN SECONDS, THE ENRAGED FURUTZ ARE SHOVING INTO THE FLOATING STATIONS ...

... DESTROYING, WITH HORRIFYING BRUTALITY, ALL THE PIPES IN THEIR WAKE ...

... BEFORE DIVING BACK BENEATH THE STRANGELY COLORED WAVES.

BARELY BEGUN, THE BATTLE DRAWS TO A CLOSE, ON A SPECTACLE OF INTENSE DESOLATION ...

AT THE SAME TIME, SOMEWHERE ALONG THE SHORE BORDERING ANANIL FOREST...

WONDERFUL, MY DEAR SON! YOU STRUCK THE FURUTZ EXACTLY WHERE I TOLD YOU, IN HIS ONLY VULNERABLE SPOT! NOW YOU TRULY BELONG TO ALFLOLOL!

WHAT DEVASTATION!

TERRAN AGENTS!

IT'S THE FAULT OF THOSE IMBECILES UP THERE ...

THE IMBECILES ARE ON THEIR WAY! DON'T MOVE AND KEEP AN EYE ON THE ALFLO... ON THOSE FILTHY NOMADS OF YOURS!

GOOD! THE GAME'S GONE ON LONG ENOUGH! THOSE SAVAGES HAVE BEEN CAUSING ONE DISASTER AFTER ANOTHER, DISORGANIZING OUR SYSTEM OF PRODUCTION ...

THAT'S NOT SO! IT'S YOU WHO ...

THAT'S ENOUGH! IN ANY CASE, THERE HAVE BEEN FURTHER DEVELOPMENTS AND THE COUNCIL HAS MADE SOME DECISIONS REGARDING THE ALFLO-LOLIANS!

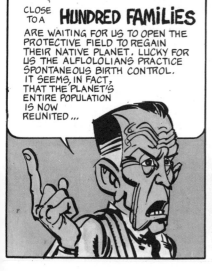

CLOSE TO A **HUNDRED FAMILIES** ARE WAITING FOR US TO OPEN THE PROTECTIVE FIELD TO REGAIN THEIR NATIVE PLANET. LUCKY FOR US THE ALFLOLOLIANS PRACTICE SPONTANEOUS BIRTH CONTROL. IT SEEMS, IN FACT, THAT THE PLANET'S ENTIRE POPULATION IS NOW REUNITED ...

AND ... THOSE DECISIONS?

THE GALACTIC CODE DOESN'T ALLOW US TO REFUSE THEM ENTRY TO TECHNOROG. IT ALSO OBLIGES US TO GIVE THEM BACK SOME LAND. WELL AND GOOD ...

BUT TECHNOROG IS ENORMOUS. LUCKILY WE CAN REGROUP THEM WITHIN AN AREA WHOSE BOUNDARIES WE DEFINE.

YOU'RE GOING TO COOP THEM UP ON A RESERVATION! THAT'S WHAT YOU'RE GOING TO DO!!

IN FACT, SEVERAL HOURS LATER, AMID THE UPROAR AND CONFUSION OF A LONG CARAVAN FLANKED BY TERRAN GUARDS AND CRAFT...

THIS IS IT! ALL THIS IS YOURS, AS FAR AS THE EYE CAN SEE!

BUT THESE ARE THE WORST HUNTING GROUNDS ON ALL ALFLOLOL!!!

AND THOSE HOUSES SMOKING OVER THERE WILL SCARE AWAY THE GAME.

AND WHILE ALL THE TERRAN CRAFTS EXCEPT THOSE CHARGED WITH THE SURVEILLANCE OF THE ALFLOLOLIAN CAMP RETURN TO THE CITY...

·YOU NOMADS ARE NEVER SATISFIED! ANYWAY... IF YOU HAVE ANY COMPLAINTS, SEE YOUR BENEFACTOR, VALERIAN! MYSELF, I HAVE TO GET BACK TO TECHNOROG. INDUSTRY WON'T WAIT! YOU CAN UNDERSTAND THAT, CAN'T YOU?...

I WOULDN'T BE SO PROUD OF MYSELF IF I WERE YOU! WHEN I THINK THAT YOU'RE CHARGED WITH ADMINISTERING THIS...

WHAT DO YOU WANT? THE ALFLOLOLIANS TRUST ME. AND WHAT'S MORE, IT'S ONLY A PROVISIONAL APPOINTMENT...

THAT'S NO EXCUSE FOR YOU TO GO ALONG WITH THIS FARCE!

IT'S TRUE, YOU REALLY DO HAVE A NEGATIVE ATTITUDE! THERE'S ENOUGH ROOM ON ALFLOLOL FOR EVERYBODY!

A LITTLE LATER, IN THE GUBERNATORIAL PALACE ...

AND IN THE SIROCCO WHICH CONTINUES TO BLOW ...

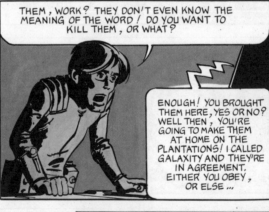

BESIDES, IT'D BE BETTER IF YOU JUST BEAT IT, WITH ALL THE GUARDS, WE DON'T NEED ANOTHER SPY. ANYWAY, NO ONE WANTS YOU HERE ANYMORE... ME, I'M GOING TO STAY AND LIVE LIKE THEM...

COME ON, MY SWEET LITTLE GOUMOUN, WE'RE GOING TO WORK, THE TWO OF US...

BUT...

BAH! IT'S A DOG'S LIFE...

I'LL GO SET UP MY DOME AROUND HERE AND WAIT. WHAT ELSE CAN I DO? I'M NO LONGER REALLY NEEDED...

SO SOMEWHERE IN THE MOST DESOLATE PART OF THE GREAT ALFLOLOLIAN DESERT, WHILE THE PLANET'S LONG NIGHT FALLS, THE ARTIFICIAL DAYS GO SLOWLY BY INSIDE A BADLY TENDED DOME...

UNTIL...

TECHNOROGVILLE CALLING VALERIAN!...

YEAH!

YOU AGAIN! GET LOST!!!

YOU'RE FORGETTING YOURSELF, YOUNG MAN. BUT I'LL LET IT PASS FOR NOW BECAUSE YOU'RE GOING TO BE USEFUL TO ME ONE LAST TIME. I'LL BE WAITING FOR YOU AT THE PLANTATIONS AS SOON AS YOU CAN GET THERE. A CATASTROPHE HAS OCCURRED. OVER AND OUT.

A CATASTROPHE? WHAT SORT OF CATASTROPHE? BAH, ONWARD VALERIAN. WHATEVER YOU DO, YOUR GOOSE IS COOKED. SO...

41

NEAR THE PLANTATION...

UH-OH!

... AND AT THE SCENE OF THE CRIME ...

OH, OH! SO THERE YOU ARE, YOU'VE COME BACK, FRIEND! WHAT DO YOU SAY TO THIS? IT'S ALREADY MORE HOSPITABLE, DON'T YOU THINK?

UH....

AND GUESS WHO TRANSFORMED ALL THOSE NASTY PLANTS INTO PRETTY FLOWERS? ... MY SON, LAGOR ...

HENCEFORTH, HE SHALL BE KNOWN AS HE-WHO-HAS-THE-GIFT-OF-MAKING-UGLY-THINGS-BEAUTIFUL!

THAT'S NICE, ARGOL ... BUT ... UMM ... IS THAT STUFF EDIBLE?

EDIBLE? YOU'RE JOKING! ANYWAY, WHAT THE TERRANS WERE PRODUCING BEFORE WAS SO AWFUL IT DOESN'T MAKE MUCH OF A DIFFERENCE!

AGENT VALERIAN, THE GOVERNOR IS WAITING TO SPEAK TO YOU.

I'M COMING, 'M COMING...

WELL...

HAVE YOU SEEN WHAT THOSE FLEABAGS OF YOURS HAVE DONE? TECHNOROGVILLE IS ON THE VERGE OF FAMINE, THERE ARE MUTTERINGS OF REVOLT. THE COUNCIL HAS MET AGAIN AND WE'VE MADE SOME NEW DECISIONS ...

TELL ME ABOUT IT, GOVERNOR, I CAN TELL THIS IS GOING TO BE ANOTHER STROKE OF GENIUS.

NONE OF YOUR WISE CRACKS. THE POINT IS TO DIVIDE UP THOSE SPACE BUMS IN A RATIONAL AND USEFUL WAY FOR THE COMMUNITY.

MAYBE IF WE SPLIT THEM UP WE'LL BE ABLE TO USE THEM MORE EFFICIENTLY. AFTER ALL, THEY'RE CLEVER AND STRONG. HERE'S WHAT WE'VE DECIDED. A THIRD OF THEM WILL GO TO THE MINES, A THIRD TO THE FACTORIES, AND A THIRD TO THE POWER PLANTS ...

IT'S UP TO YOU TO ENFORCE THESE MEASURES AND FAST ...

I REFUSE ...

OH, YOU REFUSE, DO YOU? ... I'LL HAVE YOU KNOW THAT I HAVE HERE A MESSAGE FROM GALAXITY DISMISSING YOUR FRIEND LAURELINE FOR HER INJUSTIFIABLE CONDUCT IN THE COMPANY OF THAT STELLAR TRASH SHE SEEMS TO HAVE ADOPTED ...

I CAN MAKE USE OF THIS MESSAGE ... OR NOT. IF I DO USE IT, SHE'LL FINISH HER DAYS IN THE MINES! NO MORE COZY SPACESHIPS COURTESY OF THE SPATIOTEMPORAL SERVICE FOR HER!

LAURE-LINE! THAT'S BLACKMAIL!!!

ALL RIGHT. I'LL FOLLOW ORDERS. THE MINES, FACTORIES, POWER PLANTS ... PRODUCTION'S GOING TO PICK UP STEAM, I CAN TELL!

SPARE ME YOUR COMMENTS ... AND REMEMBER, ALL OF TECHNOROG'S GUARDS WILL BE AT YOUR DISPOSAL TO CARRY OUT ORDERS. HEADQUARTERS HAVE BEEN SET UP FOR YOU. BE SO GOOD AS TO STAY IN THEM ... AND TRY TO LOOK A BIT MORE LIKE ONE OF GALAXITY'S REPRESENTATIVES ...

YOU GOT IT ...

A LITTLE LATER, WHILE THE UNFORTUNATE ALFLOLOLIANS START OUT ON YET ANOTHER EXODUS ...

LET'S GO! HURRY IT UP, YOU BUNCH OF FLEABAGS!

LAURELINE, DEAR LAURELINE, LET ME EXPLAIN ...

DO YOU KNOW THAT MAN, GOUMOUN MINE? COME ALONG, WE'RE LEAVING FOR THE FACTORIES.

BAH ... WHEN EVERYTHING GOES WRONG ...

YOUR CRAFT IS READY FOR THE TOUR OF INSPECTION AND THE GOVERNOR WISHES TO REMIND YOU THAT HE'S WAITING FOR YOU AT TECHNOROGVILLE AT THE CONCLUSION OF YOUR TOUR...

I KNOW, LET'S GO...

AND...

HERE ARE THE FIRST FACTORIES...

WHAT'S THEORETICALLY MANUFACTURED HERE?

ROCKETS, SPACESHIPS...

ARE YOU SURE? LET'S GO DOWN AND HAVE A LOOK...

AH! WE'VE BEEN WAITING FOR YOU! IT'S DREADFUL! EVERYTHING SEEMS TO HAVE GONE CRAZY! LOOK AT THE GHASTLY THINGS WHICH ARE COMING OFF OUR ASSEMBLY LINES...

MMMM YEAH ... FUNNY!

WHAT DO YOU MEAN, FUNNY? IT'S TRAGIC...

THERE'S ONE FAMILY IN PARTICULAR WHICH STANDS OUT DUE TO ITS EXTRAORDINARY ILL WILL OR APPALLING INNOCENCE...

DON'T TELL ME WHICH, I CAN ALREADY GUESS! THERE'S A TERRAN GIRL WITH THEM, RIGHT?

OH YES! TELL ME ABOUT IT, SHE'S...

TELL ME, RATHER, SINCE YOU'RE IN CONTACT WITH TECHNOROG'S OTHER INDUSTRIAL COMPLEXES... HOW ARE THEY GETTING ALONG ELSEWHERE?

TERRIBLE, EVERYWHERE! AT THE ATOMIC WEAPONS PLANT, ALL THEY CAN PRODUCE ARE POCKET KNIVES...

... AND AT THE BIOLOGY CENTER THEY ALL HAVE HAY FEVER...

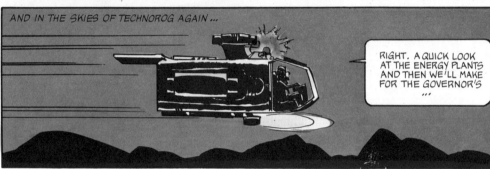

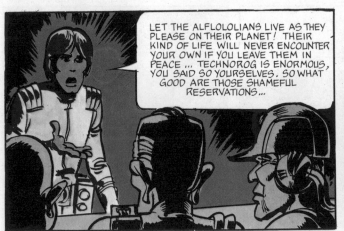

LET THE ALFLOLOLIANS LIVE AS THEY PLEASE ON THEIR PLANET! THEIR KIND OF LIFE WILL NEVER ENCOUNTER YOUR OWN IF YOU LEAVE THEM IN PEACE ... TECHNOROG IS ENORMOUS, YOU SAID SO YOURSELVES. SO WHAT GOOD ARE THOSE SHAMEFUL RESERVATIONS ...

I ADMIT ... HMM ... THAT WE HAVE ENVISIONED THAT POSSIBILITY, SINCE WE NO LONGER HAVE MUCH OF A CHOICE, WOULD YOU AGREE TO CARRY SUCH A MESSAGE TO THEM IMMEDIATELY? THEY'LL BELIEVE YOU.

UH ... I HOPE SO ...

LEAVE THEN! YOU CAN EVEN TAKE YOUR PERSONAL CRAFT TO SAVE TIME ...

AND DON'T FORGET, YOUNG MAN, OUR PRODUCTION IS IN YOUR HANDS! EVERY MINUTE LOST COSTS US A FORTUNE ...

A LITTLE LATER, IN THE EVER-DARK SKY OF ALFLOLOL/TECHNOROG ...

LAURELINE'S THE ONE WHO'S GOING TO BE REALLY HAPPY! ACCORDING TO THE RADIO, THEIR MISCHIEF DONE, THE ALFLOLOLIAN'S HAVE ALL GONE BACK TO THEIR RESERVATION. THAT'S WHERE I'M GOING TO TELL THEM THE GOOD NEWS!

THERE'S THE RESERVATION, BUT...

WHAT'S THIS? THEY'RE ALL LEAVING! WHAT AM I GOING TO DO? ...

THERE! A FEW LEFT ... GOT TO LAND, QUICK!

44 B

HOW ARE YOU, FRIEND?

WELL, HELLO, STRANGER!

WHY DID THEY ALL LEAVE? AND I WAS JUST COMING BACK TO ANNOUNCE THAT THEY WERE FREE AGAIN ON ALFLOLOL.

FREE ON ALFLOLOL! FREE ON A PLANET LIKE THIS! POOR VALERIAN, YOU REALLY DON'T UNDERSTAND A THING! THEY ALL LEFT BECAUSE THEY NO LONGER WANT ANY PART OF THEIR PLANET AND IF WE STAYED BEHIND IT WAS BECAUSE ARGOL AND HIS FAMILY NO LONGER HAVE A SHIP...

BUT, BUT...

COME ON, YOU'LL GET OVER IT, MY BOY. IN YOUR OWN WAY YOU DID WHAT YOU COULD ... BUT IT WAS THE WRONG WAY, THAT'S ALL ...

WHAT IF ... WHAT IF I TOOK YOU ALL WITH IN MY CRAFT? AND IF I GUIDED THE OTHERS THROUGH THE CHANNEL? AND IF ...

OH, I DIDN'T EXPECT ANY LESS OF YOU ...

MMMM. THAT'S MY VALERIAN, ALL RIGHT!

AND SOON, IN THE DANGEROUSLY CONGESTED VICINITY OF THE PLANET, A LONG CONVOY IS MAKING ITS WAY TOWARDS SPACE ...

47